THE GIRL IN THE SHADOWS

TAMEKA HILL

THE GIRL IN THE SHADOWS. Copyright ©
2025. Tameka Hill.

All rights reserved. No portion of this book may be
reproduced, stored in a retrieval system, or
transmitted in any form or by any means—
electronic, mechanical, photocopy, recording,
scanning, or other—except for brief quotations in
critical reviews or articles, without the prior
written permission of the author.

www.clevelandomcleish.com

ISBN-13: 978-1-965635-19-3 (paperback)

Dedicated to my parents, Evral and Dorothea Hill, for always believing in me. Whether my dreams were small or big, you've never placed them in the shadows.

contents

Strangers Bound By A Cord 3

A Saddlebag Of Secrets 13

From Enemy To Saviour 23

Happy To Die 29

Her Eyes Told Her Story 39

You're A Strong One 45

A Glimpse Of Freedom 51

The Office 57

What Is My Story? 65

Acknowledgments 73

About the Author 75

THE GIRL IN THE SHADOWS

TAMEKA HILL

strangers bound by a cord

The stench was unbearable. Aggressively, it latched to their nostrils like a larvae amphibian. Shit-encrusted floors cushioned their blue-black bodies that glistened with sweat, blood, and tears. The heat emanating from the hard iron surface created the perfect feel of being drought in the rain. It sucked their skins dry, causing their lips to crinkle beneath the seemingly white paste that covered it.

Anya sat quietly with her eyes closed and her head hung, breathing deeply as saliva mixed with blood drizzled from her bruised lips. Splatters of red fluid decorated her blue and white blouse; she examined the liquid which had formed a pattern on her chest. Staring into the darkness, she tried desperately to come to terms with this new place she found herself, but the events that occurred before remained nebulous. She lifted her head slowly, which pounded aggressively like a taiko drum being slammed violently by a bachi. Trying to gather her thoughts, she attempted to pull herself in an upright position, moving her arms to do so. Then there it was: a swift, sharp, shocking pain. In response to the surreal surge of discomfort, her toes curled, her eyes flickered, and her brows knitted as the pangs of discomfort shot through her body. She tried again, this time moving slowly. She wiggled her wrist and felt an intensifying grasp akin to a big clamp gripping and pulling on her arms.

Bit by bit, she turned her head carefully to look over her shoulder. Then, she saw it: an iron-rusted manacle clinching on her wrist, the chains interlocking with that of another young woman. Sitting back-to-back, their vertebral column lightly pressing against each other, body fluids becoming one, the only source of which provided movement sans pain.

She tried again, slowly wiggling her right hand and the side of her body. It was an effort in futility met with increasing agony, even at the slightest of force. Anya's breathing accelerated; the tympanic heartbeat sounded like a blacksmith's hammer against a cold metal. She felt it, her throat tightening, the iron walls caving in on her. The stifled sensation was expressed in the form of shaking; an uncontrollable quivering of her whole being. A lump was beginning to form in the back of her throat restricting the airway. Her eyes began to bulge, her cheeks puffed, holding hostage carbon dioxide, which desperately sought to create a route of escape. It was about to happen, the loud, terrifying scream that normally accompanied her panic attack.

"Oyi! Oyi!"

The voice was loud and harsh, putting a dead holt on Anya's bout of anxiety.

"Weh yah do deh no mek no sense. Just sit dung and stop di bag a moving, cause yuh ongle a mek mi chain get tighter wid you madness."

It was the girl with whom she shared a fetter. Her patois was intense; the grating weight on the pronunciation of each vowel told her story. She was from a deep rural part of Jamaica, Saint Elizabeth perhaps. Judging from her speech, it was obvious she lived with her grandparents or grew up around aged folks, as the vernacular "oyi" is not popular amongst young Jamaicans or even the middle-aged. Though their eyes met only but halfway, Anya could see the extreme contempt with which she looked at her, and for a moment, she remained still. Her dark chocolate skin made her eyes pop; her features more pronounced as they delicately peeped through the hanging dreadlocks that graced her face.

Engulfed by the darkness, they sat silently. The quiet was often tainted with small whimpers of discomfort, sniffles, and a cough every once in a while. There were other people there. How many? She was unsure, as it was too dark to tell. Anya shuffled lightly, hoping not to upset her 'back' mate, who took small, quick glances with each move before reciprocating. Two strangers bound by a cord, in need of each other to relieve their pain, though minute.

"Me feel like me and yuh a go have some serious issue enuh gyal."

The back mate had now unwillingly become a recipient of Anya's weight, the consequence of her decision to find comfort in the discomfort. Hissing, she breathed loudly, tilting her head back, her locks shifting to reveal bruises on her lips. The marks were the product of a fork heated over a flame. The utensil had been placed squarely on her lips after she adamantly refused to partake in the 'gift of sustenance.' The punishment achieved its desire as she preferred consuming what looked like duck fetus mixed with maggot cheese than suffer further distortion.

The confined air bred many fevers and fluxes. The excessive heat that emanated from the dark iron floor, decorated with blood, mucus, and bodily excretion, has seen several victims. The first was a nine-year-old girl. Her death was quick and tortuous, as her asthma, grappling with the overpowering high temperatures, stench, and foul air, placed her in a chokehold. She gasped for air. Surrounded by screams and cries, her eyes rolled back, and she collapsed onto the plank, pulling her 12-year-old sister down with her. Unable to see her baby sister's face, confined by chains that saw them seated with their backs against each other, she screamed uncontrollably, tears decorating her face. She spent what seemed like eons there, on the floor, lying in the piss of her dead sister. Incapable of looking at her one last time, she held on to the only thing that had meaning: her little finger. It was cold and lifeless. After her sister's body was removed, she fell silent, only humming softly as she rocked back and forth.

The nine-year-old was only the beginning, as another four also fell victim, three succumbing to the circumstances and illnesses, and the other choosing her own way of escape. A sharp protruding metal was her saviour. She dragged herself to the distended iron, grating her neck hard against it until it slit open her throat. Choking on her own blood, her death only but imminent. Between death and the unknown, she chose the darkness that was familiar, a place of safety, the promise of order and stability compared to the mystery that awaited. She chose death because the shadows brought with it hunters that hounded without reason or purpose. Indeed, the known was a better solace than ignorance. The known was best, and death seemed a more pleasant reality for her.

Anya squinted her eyes so they could adjust to the darkness. As her vision altered, a silhouette glistened in the darkness. Sitting right in front of her in a black crop top and a short lime green mini-skirt was the girl in braids. Her head was tilted backward; she could be no more than sixteen years old or maybe fifteen, the same age as Anya. She looked relatively calm, almost as though she was completely unaware of the circumstances around her. As Anya stared at her, she wondered, *"Is this place a figment of my imagination? Am I dreaming? I must be because there is no way anyone could be this calm in a place like this. Look at her!"*

Her thoughts decorated her face as they ran wild like mad cattle on a highway. The girl with braids, as though she had a front-row ticket in Anya's mind, returned her stare before asking,

"A wha? Weh yah look pon me so fah? Yuh never see pum pum before?"

Anya looked away quickly, stunned by her question. The girl with braids chuckled, adjusting her legs so Anya could see a small protruding stomach lightly hung over her exposed pudenda. Turning her gaze towards the ground, her brows furrowed. Anya breathed slowly, then in hushed tones said, "This is a dream. This is a dream." Her mother had taught her this breathing routine when she had her first panic attack at ten years old. Her kitten, Sally, had fallen to her demise after her father caught the pet stealing the flat of a fried chicken wing he had placed in a dish on the cupboard. Rife with anger, he screamed at the black and white kitten, which he hurled at before throwing her through the window. Bones too weak to support her, Sally fell and broke her neck.

"Breathe," her mother cautioned as Anya fought the tears that sought desperately for freedom. Overwhelmed by her own emotions, she tried to circumnavigate between anger and understanding. It was pointless and only resulted in the feeling of suffocation as she clutched her throat, which was muffled with trapped air.

"Come on, sweetie, just breathe for mommy," her mother admonished again, with such softness and tenderness only a psychologist would be capable of.

"Breathe..."

With her mother's kind speech riddled with affection and concern, Anya opened her mouth, releasing her breath accompanied by a huge crashing scream. Falling to the floor, her little yellow tutu dress, a gift from her father, covered her small legs; she bawled uncontrollably, her body shaking violently.

Heeding to the sound of her mother's voice in her head, she closed her eyes and breathed slowly, her lips slightly parted. The air passed through her mouth with a fragile yet determined force. She recoiled, gagging at the stench of her own breath and throwing her head to the left to avoid it.

"Oyi! Look yah nuh girl, a nuh hotel u deh, so nuh bother wid the bag a breathing cause u mouth stink like wha!" Her backmate screamed at her in disgust.

The girl with braids looked across at her, her eyes dark. She smiled, menacingly and mockingly. Anya did not look away; she stared right back, angry at her indifference and calm. As the girl with braids broke her stare, Anya turned her gaze downward, thinking deeply about what this all was. Suddenly, she noticed a warm, yellowish-orange liquid creeping towards her feet. Anya stared at the fluid inches away from her toes. It reeked of ammonia; it was there that she realised it was piss. She tried to lift her feet to avoid it, but the shackles, firmly pinned in place, pulled against her leg with even greater force. A small ant walking leisurely across the hardened iron floor was its first victim. It fought hard, its little legs moving with such alacrity and strength. Sadly, however, it was not enough, as the intensity of the liquid flushed over it. Anya, never one to give up, tried again to lift her feet, but pain shot through her leg like ripples in water, causing her to groan. With stubborn determination, she lifted her toes, hoping it would be enough. But it was too late. The urine engulfed her toes, soaking her bare feet. She looked down in disgust, wondering who could be so filthy.

"A likkle pee-pee never hurt nobody enuh."

It was the girl with braids. With a smug grin decorating her face, she winked at Anya and blew her a kiss.

Anya's nose flared, her anger taking root, her lips quivered.

"You are so disgusting" were the only words that escaped her mouth. Frightened by her own voice, her right eye twitched, her jaw clenching as her muscles tensed.

"Ha!" The girl with braids declared, her eyes rounded, her smile bright,

"An' di likkle uptown girl speaks," she said, mocking Anya's voice and tone.

"Lisa, stop man. All a dis nuh necessary," a voice pierced through the darkness, commanding and strong. Anya looked towards her left. The voice seemed to have emanated from the girl hutched in the shadows, alone, her hands and legs seemingly free. She was thin and tall. Though her face was hardly visible, there was a beauty and elegance about her. She wore a white dress, soiled, the sleeve slightly torn, but somehow remained graceful. The girl with braids, Lisa, rolled her eyes, tilting her head backward yet again, as she bellowed a low but quite audible, "Ahhhh?!"

a saddlebag of secrets

A new day dawned, and everything remained a blur. The smell of urine and putrid menstrual blood covered the air like a hot, dirty blanket. Anya's breathing was hoarse and heavy, and an unusual, murky taste lingered in her mouth. She was hungry and desirous of a bath. As she tried again to understand the nothingness before her, she realised her efforts were only futile, as her brain was moving slower than an artic glacier.

Lost in the darkness, Anya's mind conjured up the perfect escape. She recalled the last time laughter had overtaken her, her pent-up breath escaping in snorts that only fuelled the hilarity. Only Chris, her closest friend, could elicit such unrestrained laughter from Anya. Chris was always game for Anya's antics, whether it was a harmless prank or a well-crafted joke. His tales had a cinematic quality as if they were plucked from a screenwriter's imagination.

"Anya," Chris whispered, "Hurry up and take them out nuh."

Anya carefully searched through the heap, removing each item as she found them with great precision and care. They were small gold beads her mother had bought to decorate the table located in the middle of the living room. It had become commonplace as a centrepiece at each Christmas dinner, and not having it would be deemed almost a cardinal sin. Now, Anya needed them for the cake she had made for Amy and John, her dolls. Like her parents, the lovebirds lived in Cherry Gardens and had the same professions: a Psychologist and a Businessman. Anya and Chris were 'asked' to make a cake for their eighteenth wedding anniversary. Amy was a stickler for the finer things of life and insisted beads be on her cake. Whether or not she could eat them was a completely different story, but for now, Anya needed to get it right.

In Anya's mind, she was moving as quickly as she possibly could, but all Chris could see was a slow-motion version of that, and with the removal of each bead, she went a bit slower.

"Anya, move faster. Mavis will be back here soon! Remember what she said?"

"Stop! You're making me nervous!" Anya responded, visibly annoyed by her friend's impatience.

Anya's heartbeat echoed in her ears like an auditory cocoon. She needed to get as many as she could without being caught. Mavis had warned that she would inform Mr. Paul, Anya's father, if they were caught making 'one more a dem cake deh.' Anya and Chris understood the implications of this, but Mavis needed to also understand that a cake without beads, particularly gold beads, was no cake at all.

"Pass them to me," Chris said as he pushed them into a small bag that hung from his neck. It was his saddlebag of secrets because no one knew what was in

it, but Chris always had it with him. Anya once joked that he perhaps had a bath with it wrapped around his neck. He said nothing, only smiled, which caused Anya to believe her claim to be true. A bag was as good as any appendage.

Once, Anya was almost a beholder to this rucksack of treasure. It was during one of his regular evening visits. He had come by to see her after a long, arduous day. It was no inconvenience, really, as he lived only two houses away. His parents, Mr. and Mrs. Bogle, were also very good friends with the Paul's; no wonder the two had grown to be so close, having known each other from as young as two years old.

Chris had fallen asleep on the small chair on the patio again. It was almost commonplace for him to doze off on his Sunday evening visits, a repercussion of what he deemed "boys' night" from which Anya was excluded. It was really just football, but his intent to ensure she knew as little as possible about what occurred was an enigma that had given rise to much speculation in Anya's mind. Her curiosity peaked to the heights of frustration as she searched for clues as to what was done at these 'boys' night' and with whom.

That day, his snore fest had given way to opportunity. He had more fun than he could have imagined and was now too tired to even think. Exhaustion had created an opening for Anya to make her perfect discovery, a cruel reprisal for having been banned from the games. The bag was in itself a great temptation, hanging loosely from his neck outside the comfort and protection of his covering. On tiptoes, Anya walked towards him. The light on his face made him appear so saintly. His caramel-toned skin glowed as the sun tenderly caressed it. His skin was always bright, perhaps courtesy of his mother, who always ensured he wore sunscreen before leaving the house and that he 'moisturise, moisturise, moisturise.' Guess it's the Dermatologist in her.

Anya cautiously approached the pouch, her fingers closing around the hook that secured the bag. She tugged at it slowly, but it seemed so perfectly hitched that she could not pull it apart. She breathed calmly; composure was necessary for a task as great as this. It was now or never, and with this resolve, she tried again. Lifting the hook from the eye, the rust of the metals made a loud clicking sound reverberating throughout the open space. How loudly it banged amidst the slow, calm wind and onto her ears. Chris moved his head slowly, turning it away from the light. This was perfect and gave her a better chance to make a quick entry. As she pulled open the small bag, she felt a slow rush of victory, lightly flicking her tongue upward, touching the right side of her top lip, her mouth curved, forming a wry grin. Turning his head, Chris' big, bright eyes met Anya's.

"What are you doing?" he asked, looking down at her hand, then towards her face. She ogled at him in fear and shame. She thought of running, but her legs were frozen. It was as though the mortar had swallowed her in revenge for her intrusion. She tried to open her mouth to speak, but only air was expelled from her lips. Staring at him, Anya choked the laugh, and before long, they were both laughing at her effort and its failure.

"Anya!" Chris' screamed, muffled by a whisper, "Pass them to me quick. She's coming!"

Pushing the drawer back in place, she ran from behind the kitchen cupboard, passing the beads to Chris while pulling Amy and John under her arms. Throwing the beads in his bag, Chris quickly walked towards the passageway, his hands firmly clasped behind his back.

"Weh di two a unnu up to now?"

It was Mavis. She was a stout woman, her hair always in two cornrows, neatly kept. Towering over them, she reached for a cloth hanging loosely from her skirt, using it to wipe her visibly wet hands. With each rub, she shifted her gaze from one to the other, unspoken words exchanging between them. They smiled nervously, trying to convince Mavis they were *two darling angels sent upon the earth to perform the Lord's work. They needed to be convincing that they had heeded Mavis' constant caution about making cakes, an act Mr. Paul considered a grand waste of time, not to mention 'an unprofitable business venture.'*

The truth was, despite Amy and John's well-kept physique and fancy home, they had no money; no money at all. Anya jerked her arm back and forth, sending her customers further up her armpit. This was it for sure. If Mavis told Mr. Paul, then her ass would be sore for eternity, so sore her children would behold it and ask, "Mama, why is your rear blue?"

And she would lie and tell them she painted it that way. She would prefer a fine spanking than her parents' disappointment. To be cursed into oblivion is far worse than a blue ass, as a sore rump can heal, but their disappointment and words echoing same would scar deeper than the human eye can ever see.

"Come wid me," Mavis said, as she pulled them both by their hands, walking towards the patio, then outside heading to the cherry tree at the back of the house. Anya pulled from her grasp, running towards the tree before standing in front of it. Chris looked down. Mavis' eyes squinched as she stared at Anya, who was no older than nine at the time, well, nine and a half, as Anya often corrected.

'Move!" Mavis said, pushing Anya away.

There it was, a cake made of dirt, covered in white foam, with a small cherry placed square in the middle. Oddly, the smell of the wet dirt, mixed to perfection, was heavenly. Amy and John would be pleased.

"Unnu still a mek this mud cake foolishness?"

Mavis asked, looking at the children who hung their heads in shame.

"Weh you get icing from?" Mavis questioned as she looked at the cake.

"It's rrrrfrompah."

"Wha?"

Mavis said, turning her ears to the left to make sense of the words coming from Anya's mouth.

"It's daddy's shaving cream."

There was silence. The stout woman's eyes rounded, her brows furrowed. She stared at the small children; their heads held down while their beady eyes peered up at her. Then, out of nowhere, Mavis bellowed a huge laugh. Arching her back, she slammed her hands on her thigh and screamed, "Lawd Jesas!" She squealed, her shoulders jerking to and fro as she cackled. Out of breath, Mavis clutched her stomach, her laughter subsiding into chuckles. She wiped away a tear with a gentle touch, a soft smile playing on her lips.

"Unnu business a gwaan, man. So how much fi dis now? Cause it affi dare fi look so nice," she said, completely entertained. "Doe mek it happen again,

yuh hear." The two nodded their heads in unison before Mavis walked away, chuckling to herself as she did.

Anya and Chris stared at each other, smiling. They exhaled.

from enemy to saviour

The Girl in the Shadows

A loud bang echoed; from the front or the back, this was unclear. Startled, Anya gazed at the area from which the sound bellowed. There was no movement amongst them; everyone remained still. Listening acutely, she heard the clanging of chains and the loud clunking of metals. There was a jarring squeak before the iron door flung open. The light hit them hard, drowning out the darkness. The air circulated the space as it rested on their faces.

As Anya surveyed the area, she could see each of them clearly. The girl in the shadows was even more beautiful than she thought. She had a perfect posture as she delicately rested her back against the iron wall. Her legs were crossed, the left one now firmly held in place by a chain. Anya remained shackled to her backmate; the other girls were now by themselves, only manacles attached to their ankles. There were approximately twelve of them, all girls, between the ages of thirteen and eighteen, but no older. Small-bodied teenagers, some more curvaceous than others, but largely slender in frame.

There were four rectangular sponges, about five feet long in length. It would appear only the older girls were possessors of this 'luxury,' the girl in the shadows being one of them. The others had layers of clothing in a stack formed in the shape of a small pillow. The perfect quadrilateral shapes carved into the iron floor revealed it was a metal container, the ones often used to transport goods on large ships. It was hollow, the frames thick, and its surface decorated with bits of blood, some seemingly bigger in shape and form. At each corner were small pails, a roll of tissue laid perfectly beside them.

Two men stood in the way of the light, silhouettes of their bodies formed, their faces unclear. As one walked towards them, his physique broad, strong, and firm, the young girls made muffled shrieks and cries, stained with fear and hopelessness.

"Andrew, she wake up enuh," the man said, looking at Anya.

He strolled towards her, smiling as he did. His desert boots planked itself in the small puddle of urine that lingered still. As he stooped down, he stared at her, grabbing her face with the thick of his hand. He slowly moved it back and forth, inspecting it as though it were a fruit being checked for ripeness. She grimaced as she tried to pull herself away from his grasp.

"Yuh pretty though," he said, running his thumb across her thin lips.

She cowered under his touch. His thick mustache, as copious as a blanket of snow, curled as he pulled his face closer to hers. As he placed his hand on her left inner thigh, Anya felt chills, her breathing heavy. It could all be in her mind, but her body was heavy, lifeless. Was she dead? She stared at his fingers, slowly moving up and down her thigh. Her ability to move—

impossible. She looked away, her face flushed with trepidation and humiliation. She glanced through the corner of her eyes to see if his gaze remained affixed. It lingered still. Removing his arm from her thigh, he moved his fingers stealthily up to her chest. Lightly, he caressed her breast, making circular motions where her nipple should be. She snarled.

"Please, stop it!"

Her response was what he desired. He found her feistiness sensual, as captivating as her youthful body. Parading his broad shoulders and manly chest, as wide as an open road, he swung his head back and bellowed a hearty laugh.

"Yow, yow!" It was the other man, an older man. His features were strong.

"Nuh bother wid that enuh," he hissed, while he silently uttered, "Whappen to deh boy yah man!"

"A jus' likkle joke me a run with her. Weh yah gwa'an so fah? Me nah do her nothing," Ryan declared. Looking back at Anya, he asked, "Yuh hungry?"

It was odd, but that one question about her well-being allowed Anya to 'see' him. He was no older than twenty-five years old, maybe twenty-seven. He was attractive, with a thick beard framing his face and his brows perfectly arched around his eyes. He wore a bluish-green cap which sported an angel wing at the front. He was never without it, as it was the perfect camouflage to hide the scar that ran across his temple.

She surveyed his outfit, his pecs dreamily sketched under an army green shirt, the armpit stained with sweat. His smell was strong, a mix of perspiration and dirt, his breath harsh.

Her eyes softened as she stared at him. *How could he be so beautiful and yet so cruel*, she thought.

"Hey!"

He broke her thought.

"Yuh hungry?"

His voice was softer, sweeter, and more tender, and she nodded her head timidly. He rested his arm on his leg, groaning faintly while raising himself up. Walking towards the open door, he beckoned to the other gentleman,

"Andrew, gimme di box food deh fi di new girl."

Returning to offer her the food, he opened it; the smell was heavenly. Though it looked unappetising, she was happy, not only because she was hungry but because she loved green bananas with curried chicken. As he took a small fork, he jammed it in the banana, severing a small part from the whole and dipping it in the curried gravy. Anya's mouth watered. He beckoned her to open her mouth as he teased her palate with small bits of food. Whether or not it was delicious is unknown, as any food would be sumptuous at this point. As she gnawed at the pieces in her mouth, she moaned as a woman experiencing a slow and beautiful orgasm at the first thrust. He smiled at her, the sounds appealing, her delight beautiful.

happy to die

The Girl in the Shadows

Anya woke up, looking around in the darkness. She was still there; it was not a dream. It was her third day in this hell hole. Everything was a blur, as she could not make sense of her new reality. Much to her surprise, Anya realised she no longer had a back mate, but was lying by herself on the cold, hard iron floor. Sitting up, her eyes widened as she realised she could now move without restriction. It was a small freedom but one for which she was grateful.

Her eyes increasingly adjusted to the darkness, and she looked towards the corner of the room. There it was, a small light blue pail, the tip sullied with pellets of shit. She raised herself, walking towards it. She heard a clanking sound; it was a chain attached to her leg, roughly three feet long, lengthy enough to take her to and from the pail. Positioning herself in a hunch, she took reign of her body, enough not to sit, but to instead perfectly squat over it. She waited; nothing came. Her breathing was hoarse and heavy. She waited, but still nothing.

"Tick, tick, tick, tick," it was the girl with braids, Lisa.

Anya ignored her, concentrating while whispering to herself, "Pee, just pee."

"Tick, tick, tick, tick," Lisa declared again before cackling like an evil villain in a movie. Ignoring her once more, she concentrated, then there it was: small trickles of urine.

Raising herself, a small stream of light broke the darkness. Resting upon her shoulder, Anya looked up towards it. It brought her such joy. As the streaming light glistened on her honey skin tone, she lifted her head to face it. She thought, "Perhaps, just perhaps this is it." Her soul was now leaving her body towards heaven. If this is what death feels like, then she was happy to die. Who knew a small ray of light could bring happiness?

"It feel nice, don't?" It was the girl in the shadows.

Her voice was soft and soothing. She had a motherly instinct about her that made you feel safe, as though you could trust her. Anya, seemingly frightened by the voice, looked towards her. She held her head as the slight movement blurred her vision.

Closer than before, Anya inched towards the girl in the shadows.

"Andrew came last night. He took the shackles off and put that chain on you. Guess him like you," she said to Anya with a gentle smile.

"Andrew nuh like nobody, a woman him want," the girl with braids retorted, her voice intense and angry.

Completely ignoring her, Anya asked timidly, "Can I sit with you?"

The girl in the shadows looked up, smiling. She patted her hand lightly on the metal surface; it echoed.

Her presence calming, her nature comforting. She turned her body away from Anya, looking towards the right of her shoulder as she reached behind her. Returning, she brought with her an orange cup. It looked old and was seemingly large with a thick handle. It was a cross between a beer mug and an old-fashioned tumbler, but plastic.

"Drink this," she urged Anya.

"What is it?"

"It's supposed to be tea, but it's probably cold by now. They took it really early this morning and then left."

Anya sipped from the orange cup; it was as sweet as nectar, but it was refreshing and just what she needed. She pulled the cup towards her lips, tilted her head back, and gulped it down. Burping, she licked her lips. The girl in the shadow laughed lightly. Anya reciprocated before resting her hand on hers while declaring, "Thank you."

Sitting in silence, thinking of how much this stranger felt like a sister, Anya thought about her own baby sister. She was three years old, but she missed her dearly. Her baby sister was the ultimate blessing. Blessing because her mother wanted so badly to give her a baby sister. She had had six failed pregnancies before; the sixth was the most devastating.

Anya was hiding outside her parents' room. Her father was standing, looking through the window, and her mother was sitting at the end of the bed crying...again. Anya's father, Damian, turned, his body facing his wife. He wore a navy blue jacket and pants, his tie undone. He sighed as he leaned against the window. He wasn't sure what to do this time. He knew this one was different; its impact was greater because this was the furthest she had come. There was such an intense connection with this one that saw them making plans. It was a little boy, Isaac, they had named him. He was stronger than the others who had only survived for two, sometimes three months. Isaac, however, was in his sixth month and was intent on not being kept a secret. Everyone was so excited for him, but no one was as excited as Anya, who would giggle uncontrollably whenever she heard her brother's beating heart.

Isaac loved his father and would often move with intense energy at just the sound of his voice. Damian was in love with the thought that he and his unborn son had already shared such an intense bond. As soon as he arrived home from work, he would greet Fae, his wife, kissed Anya on her forehead, and then he would kneel down to her stomach and whisper, "Hey, baby boy." Those three words would trigger Fae's stomach, which wiggled, moving inward and back with such swiftness. Fae giggled and moaned all at once. The sensation always made her teary-eyed, but she enjoyed it. Anya was never made aware of the reason for the failed pregnancies before. What she knew was that at ten years old, she would finally have a sibling, a baby brother.

But the speed with which Isaac moved, at which he grew, was the same speed with which he left. He gave no warning; nothing went wrong. Fae just went to the bathroom at work and realised she was bleeding. After inducing labour and being in the operating room for three hours, the doctor delivered the news to Damian and Anya, "He was gone." Though her friends and family members were concerned, Fae hated hearing them ask about her. She hated hearing his name. The more they asked, the harder it got. Retelling the story was like reliving the pain of her loss over and over again. Anya felt helpless as her mother walked around the house, an empty shell of her former self.

Damian would move towards Fae, putting his hand out to just touch her, but would always pull back, remembering the last few times he did, only to be told, "No, don't touch me." Though his heart was breaking, he had to comfort his wife. But this was also his son, his male heir. He had his own perception of his relationship with his son, even visualising what he'd look like. He hoped he would look more like his wife, but he'd have the same business acumen as his father. He had hopes of teaching him how to swim, watching sports game and even having a favourite football team. It could be any team but Arsenal, definitely not

Arsenal. As he reflected on the little son he'd never meet, his eyes became blurry, blinded by his own tears. He wiped them away quickly, thinking, "Be strong. Your wife needs you now."

"Fae, I don't have the right words to say. I don't know what to say. Nothing I say will bring him back, I know that. But I want to be there for you, so could you please tell me what to do? Anything at all, just to help ease the pain?"

Fae looked up at him with tears in her eyes. Their marriage had been through so much, and she hadn't been the easiest to deal with, especially during the different miscarriages. She thought of how supportive and strong her husband had always been. She had never seen him cry, and he always encouraged her that God would do it for them, but in His time. She hated hearing those words, "His time." Silently, she would argue, "When is His time? Why did He have to be so selfish? Why did things have to operate on His terms? I want my baby now! Doesn't God know these miscarriages are affecting me and my marriage? Does He even know that sex is no longer an activity I enjoy, but is instead a means to an end?"

She had so many unanswered questions, but most of all, she had so much anger. She would often argue with God during her prayers, but she wasn't even interested in praying this time. She was just too tired, *too tired to fight, too tired to pray, and too tired even to live.*

She lifted her hand so she could hold on to his. Damian's brown eyes sparkled against the sunset's glow pouring in from their front window. She thought of how she must really hurt him each time she screamed at him to "Just get it over with!" How self-serving had she become?

"The loss of a child was not only affecting me. It must also affect him," she thought. Her heart broke because, somehow, she had forgotten about her partner and friend for the last twelve years. She had not been a friend to him. Instead, she was a monster. The tears rolled down her face, this time, for having a man she took for granted.

"Could you just hold me," she said in a small whisper.

"I can do that," he said as he sat beside her. She embraced him, resting her head on the pit of his shoulder. Anya stood in the frame of the door, her father looking up at her. Fae, seeing her daughter in tears, beckoned for her to come. She held her in her embrace. There was silence in the Paul's household that night. No one spoke, but so much was said.

Atiya was unplanned, a complete surprise. She was their seventh pregnancy, one which left her parents in a daze. With the many disappointments, it was understandable why they were neither anxious nor excited. They were, instead, simply existing. For most of the pregnancy, she remained nameless. Their family was mum. Fae's oversized clothing was blamed on baby weight from the previous pregnancy, despite the two-year time gap. When Atiya finally made her entrance, the world was shocked and excited by her presence. Her small body filled a wide vacuum within a home that had suffered several hits. Atiya, gift of God, was needed. She knew it and fought with everything within her to be there.

Anya was close to her sister, who called her 'Yah' because she couldn't get the full name right. Anya smiled at the memory. Even in the darkness, her memories remained her closest friend.

her eyes told her story

The Girl in the Shadows

Staring upwards in the darkness that engulfed her, Anya sighed. Looking down at her toes, covered in dirt and grime, she thought of how desperately she needed a pedicure. But a pedicure in this 'unknown' was really the least of her concerns.

"I need food, a bath, and just fresh air," she whispered aloud.

The darkness gave way to the wail of a young lady sitting to the left of the girl in the shadows. She echoed sounds of excruciating pain, a noise Anya had heard but was too confused to realise was that close to her. Laying in a yellow floral dress, decorated with drips of blood stains, her hair was uncombed and thick, with a headband pulling away the strands from her face. She moaned a bit louder, moving her legs.

"What's wrong with her," Anya asked the girl in the shadows.

"She on har period. She get really bad cramps and dis place nuh help. She soon alright though," she said consolingly.

The young woman moaned a bit louder, moving her legs, revealing a towel placed neatly between them with splatters of body fluid. Anya turned her face away, then looked towards her yet again.

A burst of laughter hit hard against the iron container. Everyone was still, even the moaning woman. The voices grew louder amidst footsteps, one sweeping, the other stern and strong. The sounds grew louder and louder. Suddenly, the door swung open, and the light pierced the dark space like an arrow in a deer's flesh. Anya squinted; they all did. Light was an unfamiliar but welcomed feeling.

"Place stink eh man!" Ryan said as he looked at the groaning woman grotesquely. He walked past her towards the smeared pail. Covering his hand in a plastic bag, he picked it up, repulsed by its content, he gagged. Andrew laughed.

"Yow, move man, cause a me did get it the last time," Ryan retorted.

Walking away with the pail, Andrew snickered at his brother, hitting him on the arms before walking towards the girls in the room. He examined each carefully.

"It come again?" he asked the moaning girl.

"Weh yuh think?" She said, her voice grainy, powerful, and brash.

Andrew smiled while continuing down the container, observing each with caution. Some of the women cowered under his stares, but not the girl with braids. She simply stared back as though she wanted him to speak to her so she could throw a fit. He didn't. He simply walked past her, not returning her gaze.

Returning with the pail, the rims still smeared, Ryan pulled his body up, jumping inside the container.

"Yuh see dat?" he called out to Andrew.

"Whappen now?"

"My yute, you nuh see how me jump in, never use the steps enuh."

"Oh, di likkle gym a work fi u!" Andrew said with a smile.

It was as his biceps bulged from beneath the forest green oxford shirt he was wearing. His matching cap shaped his chiseled jawline, his smile, heavenly.

Placing the pails in their corners, Ryan walked beside his brother, mimicking his body movements unknowingly.

"What about this one?" Ryan said, pointing at a girl dressed in jeans. She looked as though she was no older than thirteen years old. She pulled her knees to her chest, jerking back and forth, tears streaming down her face.

"She nuh ripe enough yet, man," Andrew said in response.

He was a tall man, at least 6'3" or maybe even 6'4". His accent was thick, heavy, and deep, and he slurred as he spoke. He looked to be in his early 50s, possibly late 40s, and wore his hair in cornrows. It needed a redo, as small hairs roamed free above the interlocking plaits. Towering over the girls, he pulled Anya's former backmate, the girl with dreadlocks.

"Let's use this one!" He shouted towards Ryan.

As they grabbed her arms, pulling her in unison, she screamed, throwing her legs back and forth while shaking her head vigourously. Refusing to move her legs, her body became heavy. Sensing her reluctance, they both admonished her to start walking, each pulling at her arms as though she was a stubborn animal. She hollered loudly. With this, Andrew moved towards her, and then a thud, as he used the back of his hand to slap her in the face. Splatters of blood mixed with saliva exited her bruised lips. Grabbing her arms more firmly, the brothers lifted her down the container. Tears stained her face as she seemed to stare at Anya. Her eyes told her story.

"Unnu behave unnu self. We soon come," Andrew warned.

As the light irradiated from behind him, he appeared as the shadow of death. He stared at them as his mustache curled up, forming a lopsided 'c.' He licked his lips; a spittle hung from his lower lip. He turned his back, slamming the door behind him. The clanging of metal chains and a sudden bang signaled it was locked.

you're a strong one

The truth of what this place was, was still unclear to Anya. The girl with the dreadlocks had not returned, and no one was perturbed. No one spoke; only sniffles and low moans could be heard. Anya was afraid; afraid to speak, afraid of the sound of her own voice. She did not wish to become one of them, so accustomed to this darkness she would be blinded by the light.

'Whatever this 'new world' was would never be her new existence, her new life," she told herself.

Humming could be heard throughout the container; it was the girl in the yellow dress, the one who lost her sister. It was the sound of Bob Marley's "Don't Worry." She held her head back against the container as she hummed softly. She looked relatively calm, almost as though what transpired earlier was simply a figment of their imagination.

"What is this place?" Anya asked, breaking the humming amidst the silence.

There was no answer, just silence. After waiting for a while, the girl in the yellow dress began humming again. Anya hung her head as a tear fell thunderously on the iron surface.

There was the sound of footsteps again. With each second, it grew louder and louder until suddenly, the iron door flung open, revealing Andrew. Ryan was not with him, but the girl with braids was beside him. Anya was relieved to see her former backmate, her eyes beaming with excitement. This was not returned as the look of exhaustion latched itself to her face. Her eyes dark, her breathing heavy, her mouth opened, her posture dropped. Andrew pushed her to the corner. She plopped herself on the ground, her arms outstretched, as she stared into the unknown. He attached a manacle to her ankle as she laid still, almost appearing lifeless.

"You think you bad nuh true?"

Andrew looked down at the girl with braids; she returned his stare. She did not respond, her lips pursed, her eyes squinched. He stooped down, now at her level, and smiled wryly at her before grabbing her neck and pulling her face towards his. Lisa did not react; it was as though she were dead: no emotions, no resistance, just lifeless. He hard-pressed her against the cold floor, her back now on the ground. He breathed heavily as he pushed his coarse, hard body against her small frame.

"What are you doing? Stop it!" Anya screamed at him.

"Shut up yuh raas and mine me affi come deal wid yuh," he said, with stern eyes, his voice strong. Anya's eyes were laden with tears, and the girl with braids looked at her, not mockingly but with sadness. Looking at Lisa, Anya hoped she could do something to help her, so she did the only thing she could, she smiled. A smile forged in sadness and consolation.

Andrew grabbed the face of the girl with braids so she was looking directly at him; he kissed her aggressively. Grabbing her hand, he placed it squarely on his erect cock, holding it in place. He stared at her; his eyes were as dark as a demon's dreaded thoughts.

"Is that what you want?" He asked, his lips curved into a smile. Staring at her breast, he looked at her longingly.

"A from mawning yah tease me don't," his voice muffled as he kissed her neck and chest. The girl with braids laid still, no flinching, no movement, her eyes widened, staring towards the darkness.

"This is what a man feels like," he said while he pinned her with his right hand and used his left hand to fondle her breast. Finally, she wiggled under his touch; it excited him. He broke out into a fit of laughter, forcing her against the floor harder. He slipped his slithering tongue down her throat; she choked slightly while trying to push him away. He smiled.

"Me like how yuh strong yuh see!" He exclaimed.

"A this yuh like?"

He continued as he pulled up her skirt, revealing her vagina. He pulled her legs and drew her closer to him. Anya screamed, beckoning to the girl in the shadows, then to the moaning woman, but they were silent, numb or frozen, simply watching the monster.

After struggling to pull his pants beneath his ass, the 6-foot beast forced himself inside her, moaning in ecstasy. Lisa remained unresponsive, silent. He pushed inside her harder and harder with every thrust. His thick hands grabbed the small of her hips, and he squeezed it, leaning in, always wanting more. As he breathed loudly, his breath stained with the smell of heavy liquor, he moaned. His thrusts increased, and his breathing accelerated,

"Ahhhhh," the rapist yelled in delight.

He rolled himself from on top of her before sitting upright, panting. His penis hung loose; remains of seminal fluid lingered on the tip. He smiled, his skin flushed.

"Andrew! Weh yuh do!"

The door pulled wider, revealing a high concrete wall; that was Ryan. He walked towards his brother, dragging him up, as Andrew zipped his pants, staggering as he tried to stand alone. Wiping his sweat, he said, "Sorry man, sorry but..."

"Yuh know if dem know a u breed deh girl deh dem a go kill yuh! Why you always a faas with har? Look how yuh come down hard on me when me touch di girl and u in here a sex di likkle pickney, again! A one instruction dem give we, nuh mess with the products and from deh girl deh come yuh inna har hole," Ryan chastised, breaking him off mid-sentence.

Andrew did not answer; his head hung down with a look of dejection stamped across his dark eyes. Ryan lightly shoved him, shaking his head in disappointment as he walked towards the exit. Andrew quickly followed, wiping his nose before closing the container door behind them.

As Anya adjusted her eyes to this new darkness, she stared at the girl with braids, her body unmoved and eyes wide open.

"Are you okay," Anya asked.

She did not respond. Instead, a single tear trickled down her cheek.

a glimpse of freedom

It had been approximately two weeks; Anya knew the routine. Andrew and Ryan graced the container each morning. They fed them; they returned two hours later, pulling a girl or two to a world unknown. Each day, they chose a different girl. Only one girl never returned. She was 'new,' coming in four days after Anya. She seemed to have walked straight off the runway to a container. She wore smeared mascara and a sequined green dress with gold pumps; very fashionable. She had hazel eyes and dark cascading hair, maybe hair extensions, but she was beautiful. After just one day, Andrew pulled her away, but she never returned. Anya had not been a victim of this dark, unknown world, and she prayed that day would never come.

As the small streak of light peeped through the small hole, Anya knew it was time. The footsteps approached, and Andrew and Ryan entered the container with food. This morning, it was an egg sandwich.

"Yuck," Anya thought. She was not a fan of eggs.

"Hey," Ryan said, walking towards her. "Look here!"

As Anya pulled the foil paper apart, she saw the bread. She looked at him questioningly.

"Look inside nuh," he said excitedly.

It was ham and cheese. Anya was excited. She wondered how he knew she hated eggs and why he had gone out of his way to make her something different. She felt special, and a small part of her felt as though Ryan was a safe place in an unsafe world. She felt a surge as he placed the sandwich to her mouth and she bit in.

"Hey, the chain has been pinching my ankle. Can you just loosen it a little?" she said in hushed tones.

Ryan looked towards the door. Andrew had stepped away, completely out of vision. He looked at her, his eyes timorous yet compassionate.

She whispered, "Please."

"Weh yuh mean loosen? A tek you want me tek it off?"

She smiled at him, nodding in agreement.

"It's annoying, and keeps pinching and bruising my ankle. I can't take it."

"Look here," he whispered back, "no bother wid no foolishness enuh! Me nuh supposed to do dis, but me like yuh, so if me do dis, no bother do nuh foolishness. Yuh hear?"

She shook her head violently, the others watching on, salivating at the moment and what seemed to be even a small glimpse of…freedom.

He pulled a key from the back of his pants, all the while looking towards the door of the container. Andrew was still nowhere in sight. He flickered it, his eyes filled with concern; he paused. Anya quietly whispered, "My ankles are red. Look at it. I feel like some dog in a cage."

The words seemed to have been all he needed, as with this, he began to open the manacle. As he did, she felt the loosening of the chains, and as he freed her ankle, she used her foot to lightly push the shackle to her hand. Grabbing it, she swung the manacle with full force, giving Ryan a hard blow. It hit the side of his head, his hat flying to the floor. The shock of the hit caused him to wobble.

"A weh di…" he declared, his eyes dazed.

Before he could complete the sentence, she screamed, slamming him again and again with the fetter until he fell to the floor.

"Kakafart, the uptown girl have use man!" exclaimed the girl with braids with a joyful laugh.

Anya rushed to her feet, staring at the other girls, who simply gazed, their eyes startled. She felt confused. She hadn't given it much thought. She actually gave it no thought at all; she was simply acting on impulse. She stood there bewildered. A slight groan came from the man on the floor. She looked quickly towards him and saw small movements as he struggled to get up.

"Girl! Run nuh! Weh yah wait fah? Run before Andrew come!"

It was the girl in the shadows; her hazel eyes beamed with enthusiasm.

And with that, Anya ran.

Running towards the open door, she stared at the ground, the openness, the liberty. The other girls screamed, perhaps cheering for her freedom or crying at their demise. Jumping from the container, which was raised three feet from the ground, Anya looked to her right, only to see three more containers, and on her left an additional four. "What is this place? Are more girls in these containers?" Her mind ran wild. A large, grey concrete wall stood around thirty feet high. The perfect place to hide from the public, the perfect place to cage underage girls and women in containers. The place felt all too familiar. She looked to her right again, seeing only a pathway leading to a red door about 800 metres away.

Anya ran towards the door, her heart hurtling, her breath stained with the smell of ham and cheese. The uncertainty that lingered behind this door could save her life or see her lose it. She extended her hand towards the doorknob, but she saw it moving before she could touch it. She froze as she heard a hoarse male voice call out from behind the door,

"Yes, ma'am, me understand. Me a go talk to him now," the voice said; it was Andrew.

Anya jumped, moving back quickly so she could stand between the space where the door hinge met the concrete wall. The door swung open, creating the perfect hiding space. She used her hands to cover her mouth, hoping her breathing would not be loud enough to be heard. A light wind escaped, forcing itself around the door, caressing her face, and ruffling against her matted hair. Her pupils were fully dilated, drops of sweat embellished her forehead. She was uneasy and dreaded the punishment she would receive if found.

As Andrew walked towards the container, Anya went on tiptoes, gliding against the door frame, her body fully facing his back, allowing her to watch his every move. She was inside. She made it. She breathed. But it was more complex than she thought, as in front of her stood a long, lonely pathway that seemed to lead to absolutely nothing.

the office

Increasing the pace of her steps, she walked. To her right was a small blue door; she ran towards it, opening it slowly and quietly. The door squeaked.

"Shhhh," she said as she peeped inside.

There were two offices and, the jackpot, a green door, 600 metres away from the second office. Both offices had two large glass windows that would make it hard for her to pass without being seen. As she walked towards the first door, she could hear voices; though inaudible, she knew someone was there. Bending, she slowly began creeping past the first office. She could hear her heart; it was loud, strong. She peered in the window of the first office, and there was nothing there, just an empty chair and desk: no phones, no computer.

Nothing.

"What is this place?" she thought.

Creeping towards the second office, the voices grew and could be heard much more clearly. It was a man and a woman; their conversations intermingled with the sounds of light sobs. As she inched further towards the window of the second door, her knees bruised, she could hear the male voice growing with greater intensity; it was stern and aggressive.

"Was this another victim? Can I save her? Should I have saved the other girls? But, no, I couldn't, right? I have to save myself first and then get them help?" Anya reasoned to herself. Her mind was a battlefield, a thing of beauty but also a thing of great danger.

She had now successfully passed the second office window without being seen. She just needed to creep past the door, and then she would be home free, or at least wherever the green door would lead. As she inched closer towards the door, she heard the woman's voice,

"Dis is jus' too much, too much," her voice breaking in between the words.

Anya's eyes flickered as she listened even closer. The woman continued speaking. Anya stopped; she had to go back; she must be certain. As she turned around, a strong impulse, a force, told her no, to keep going, but not knowing would eat at her forever. She needed to know. As she veered towards the room, passing the door, she slightly poked her head up enough to see inside without being seen. Her heart raced in jubilation. Anya jumped to her feet, grabbed the door aggressively, and with tears in her eyes, she stood there staring before saying, "Mom! Dad!"

Her mother, whose back had been turned, curved her body towards the open door. Screaming, she rushed towards her with euphoria. They held each other, both crying. Her mother kissed her forehead generously.

Out of nowhere, footsteps could be heard approaching. It was clear; there were at least two persons. It was Andrew. He was now aware that Anya had escaped as he saw his little brother staggering from

The Girl in the Shadows

the container, his head bruised, his eye bloodshot. As their steps grew louder, she whispered to her parents,

"Shhh…I think that's them, the guys that kidnapped me. How did you get in here? Tell me so we can leave before they catch us?"

Her parents were quiet, perhaps numbed by the whole experience? Confused?

"Mr. Paul! Mr. Paul! She knock out Ryan enuh sah. We ca'an find her!" Andrew called out loudly.

"Mr. Paul!" he screamed.

With Ryan's left hand around his shoulder, Andrew swung the door open; his eyes popped as he stared into the room. Clutching to his brother for support, a droopy Ryan befuddled, held his head, which had been plastered over in drops of blood.

Staring at her father, Anya declared,

"Dad? Dad….What…"

Before she could finish, her father took out his firearm and shot Ryan in the head. Anya grabbed her face, using her hands to cover her eyes, curling her back while crouching towards her mother's stomach. The room grew still, the echo of the shot clouding the air, everyone frozen. Ryan dropped to the floor with a heavy thud. His brother hovered over him in disbelief.

"Damn idiot," Anya's father declared, releasing a huge sigh while grabbing his head with his left arm.

As he paced the room back and forth, using the gun to lightly knock against his skull, he muttered under his breath. There was silence. Anya's cheek was stained with a single teardrop as her mother pulled her close to her side. Andrew was on his knees, his head resting in his palms, as he stared through open fingers at Ryan's lifeless body.

"All he had to do was wha? Feed her! Feed her! And a fifteen-year-old girl knock you out? Fiftteen!" Anya's father shouted at no one in particular.

"Damian," Anya's mom pleaded, her palm raised upwards and outward towards her husband,

"This is too much…Anya is our daughter. We can't do this to her. Come on now."

"Our daughter?! Talk truth, Fae! We adopted her! Listen, me done talk bout this! We have our own child now, and the additional expense nah help we. You know the plan, we send her gone a school overseas, it simple. It's the perfect time; her body is ready. Everybody tun idiot now. Dem don't remember dem job?"

He stared at Fae. He pointed towards her and said, "You get into these girls' head all the time, but you can't get a simple concept into yours?"

Acknowledging Andrew, he shouted, "You capture them. Erase any trail of their existence! And you!" He snickered angrily, pointing to Ryan's motionless body, "You take care of them for our clients or until they are sold," he shouted while slamming his hand to the table, still pacing back and forth.

"So, so, you're not my parents," Anya finally asked, "I, I don't understand,"

Looking up at her mom, she said, "You're not my mom? If you're not my mom, then, who are you?"

Mrs. Paul turned towards Anya. Her hair was in a bun, the small patch of grey hair that stood at the peak of her head hung loose, lightly framing her oval-shaped face. With her lipstick smeared, her mascara running, she placed her hand on her thigh, holding her floral skirt in place. Slightly kneeling, she met Anya at eye level and said, "I am sorry, sweetie. I didn't mean for all of this to happen. You are my child; you will always be my child, and I don't want you to think otherwise. I am really sorry; I didn't mean for this…"

"Business is business, Fae. Yuh want rich life but not what comes with it? This is our life, and yuh know what you were coming into, so get this shit over with!" Damian interrupted.

"Who are my parents then? I don't understand, please." Anya said in a whisper, tears streaming down her face. Her mother clasped her face with both hands, using her forehead to meet hers.

"Mommy," Anya said in hushed tones, "Who are you?"

Mrs. Paul opened her mouth, but no words escaped. Her lips quivered, tears and snot all running toward her chin.

"I don't know what's happening, Mommy. Please, save me. I just…"

Before she could complete her statement, Damian used his gun and slammed it against Anya's skull. She fell to the floor, hitting her head hard on the desk as she did.

Mrs. Paul screamed, mimicking Anya's fall as she stared at her unconscious daughter. Her husband grabbed her by the wrist, pulling her away from Anya's body as she hollered her daughter's name in regret and dismay. As Damian dragged his wife behind him, he yelled at a frozen Andrew, "Just clean this shit up!"

what is my story?

Her head pounded as she slowly opened her eyes. She breathed out loud; a small yawn followed. Her body felt strange, heavy; her world was spinning. The small streak of light was back. It adorned her face like a strange mole. Anya squinted before turning her head towards the darkness. She tried to pull her hand towards her face, blocking the small blinding light. There it was again, the agonising pain of the manacle and chains. Feeling it, Anya's eyes widened, and her nose flared. Her breathing pattern changed.

"Welcome back, bitch!"

It was Lisa. This time, it was not said mockingly, but with a tone of sadness and delight. Anya did not respond. She couldn't. She instead mulled the words over and over again, "Welcome back."

"To be welcomed is to be embraced; it is a return to home, a place of belonging," she thought, her face motionless and her eyes dark.

As she stared at the ground again, voices muttering around about her, she looked to her left at the girl in the shadows. She could see her clearly, even in the darkness. Anya tilted her head, trying to make sense of the words being emitted from her mouth. Though she spoke, Anya heard nothing. She simply saw her lips moving about, her words muffled, drowned by the nothingness that had become her emotion. Fixed, Anya stared into the abyss; her reality was no more.

"My entire life was a lie," she said.

Her voice, her words created a hollow in the container, which was now hushed. She looked up, staring at the girl with braids, then the girl in the shadows. She smiled, "My life was a lie," she repeated.

She shrugged, tilting her head backward. She gazed at the dark space with the small stream of light that illuminated her brown eyes. As she stared, a single tear rolled off her face and fell to the ground; it was thunderous.

"All a we have a story, honey, and none of them is pleasant. Some of us were homeless, others abandoned. A few had a good life and was simply taken. But for some a we, this container is our home. We get food and wait until freedom comes," the girl in the shadows said with such empathy yet restraint.

"Freedom? A wha dat look like?" Anya's former backmate asked in disdain.

"Being bought…whateva happen afta someone buy we mus' be better dan living in an iron box. Anything at all wud a better dan this," she answered.

Each girl spoke, recounting their own lives, their own stories. It seemed that despite it all, this new reality seemed farfetched for Anya. She was unable to connect the dots.

"How could any human being do this to someone else?" she thought. "Were we some perishable items to be used and reused at another's will? How could girls be sold into such a situation, by their own family members at that? The people set to care for and love them? How could they? How could girls be here and not be discovered by authorities, the state, and even their own families? How were girls here so long they've absolved themselves into the darkness, becoming the darkness? Did anyone know where they were? Was anyone even looking for them?"

As the bickering continued, Anya looked at the girls, their mouths moving slowly. She replayed the conversation she had with her parents... her adopted parents. She had caused the death of a man who simply chose to be kind to her, to help her. She knew nothing about him, only his name. Her body still, she searched the recesses of her mind.

"Were there any signs that the people I called mom and dad were not my birth parents? They were at all my recitals. They cheered me on, laughed at my jokes, and shared their stories. My little sister... she is not my sister? And her entrance was what they needed for my exit? If this was all a lie, then what is the truth," she asked herself.

"Ms. Fae is pure evil," Lisa declared loudly.

"Lisa!" The girl in the shadows called out, her voice stern. "Stop!"

"No, me a go talk. She wicked. This woman come a me high school come counsel me, talking bout me troubled, and she would a get me help. This is help?"

She asked, pointing towards the top of the metal container.

"When you look at her, you can't quite tell because she's so beautiful, and she could be somebody's mother, you know, even my mother," Lisa continued.

"Shaval lived in St. Elizabeth," she pointed at Anya's backmate, "and she said Ms. Fae was a friend of one of her cousins, and she visited her and her family there. Shaval started confiding in this woman enuh and she mek the girl run weh, talking bout she have a safe place for her. Safe place?" She said while she snickered in disdain.

"Lisa, just chill," the girl in the shadows said, using her hand to shield Anya, almost as though she was protecting her from Lisa's words.

Lisa was harsh and seemed as dark and cold as a benighted hemisphere. But she had seen and been through it all. She had become a regular for rich old men who wanted their dicks sucked. The taste of semen had no longer repulsed her, and emotions had become a thing of the past. That happens when you've seen and endured a life some people only see in their nightmares. That happens when you've been raped multiple times in a small space while others watch, carrying a life inside you whose future was unknown, just as much as your own. It will all crush you and cause your soul to be hushed by the silence of death.

This was Lisa's world. She wasn't simply in the darkness, she was engulfed by it.

The girl in the shadows touched Anya's knees lightly, she smiled.

"I know this is temporary; everything in life is. But you also know, some temporary things can stain you for a lifetime. My aunt selling me from me likkle, I just didn't know I was being sold. I thought these new and strange uncles scared me. But if all you've known is fear, as young as five years old, then one day fear becomes you, and you no longer see the world as dark when you are the dark," she said, looking at Anya while she spoke. The room hushed into silence.

As she recalled her experiences of being sold to the Paul's for $100,000 JMD, her eyes twinkled, "At least that's better than knowing a 50-year-old man was forcing himself inside an eight-year-old girl just for a bag of flour, sugar, and chicken back. At least Mr. Paul thought I was worth much more than that."

"Who knew you could put a price on somebody's life," Anya responded to no one in particular.

As bitterness now swamped Anya's heart, overtaking sadness and anger, Anya recited the lines, "All a we have a story." She thought about the words said by a girl dressed in a soiled white dress; a girl hidden in the shadows…her name unknown.

"Everyone has a story," she said aloud. Gaining their attention, she looked around the room with a smirk, slowly nodding as she did.

"I have no memory of getting to this strange place, this hell. I've seen a man killed in front of me. I've watched a girl being raped while others watched on in horror. Girls' bodies are simply canvasses for sexual exploitation. My future is now despondent. If everyone has a story, then, what is my story? Because I don't even know who I am. Perhaps my story is, I am no longer Anya Paul; I am a trafficking victim."

acknowledgments

I have always believed that at the end of my life, I should never have regrets, just memories. Each and every day, I work towards actualising that.

I want to thank my family and friends for their support and their help during this important journey.

I offer gratitude to Dwayne Berbick, who was kind enough to edit my book, always offering constructive suggestions. I really do appreciate your assistance.

Thank you to those who continued to encourage me in its completion during the times I felt overwhelmed and downhearted because of life. Life will sometimes do that; it will cause you to cower in the shadows of your despair, heartache, and sadness, but I am blessed to have persons in my life who are my flickering lights, the lights that have aided me in the fight against the shadows.

Thank you to each and every one of you!

about the author

Tameka Hill is a Communication and International Development Specialist with a love for the arts. As the country's Youth Ambassador, Hill advocated for victims of Human Trafficking. She remains an active advocate and has written and contributed literature on Trafficking in Person. Her work has been internationally recognised, receiving a commemorative award from Commonwealth Secretariat, Bangladesh for Women and Leadership, as well as being recognised as one of the forty emerging leaders across the Atlantic in Morocco, North Africa. With a unique blend of experience in strategic communications, social development, and project management, she is internationally networked, innovative, and resourceful. Ms. Hill is adept at communicating with clarity and diplomacy with people of diverse backgrounds.

Made in the USA
Columbia, SC
11 June 2025